UNRELIABLE WITNESS

A NOVELLA BY

ALANA TERRY

Note: The views of the characters in this novel do not necessarily reflect the views of the author, nor is their behavior necessarily condoned.

The characters in this book are fictional. Any resemblance to real persons is coincidental. No part of this book may be reproduced in any form (electronic, audio, print, film, etc.) without the author's written consent.

Scriptures quoted from THE HOLY BIBLE, NEW INTERNATIONAL VERSION®, NIV® Copyright © 1973, 1978, 1984, 2011 by Biblica, Inc.® Used by permission. All rights reserved worldwide.

www.alanaterry.com

ONE

I DIDN'T MURDER my husband. It's important to explain that from the very beginning. There are enough people in the world right now who think I'm a conniving murderess. I don't need you to be one of them.

I didn't murder my husband. Which, now that I write the words out, now that I see them there on the page in front of me, they don't absolutely ring true.

You've heard of the unreliable narrator, I assume. It's a literary device. Meant to trick readers.

I read a book like that once. It was written like a detective novel, which to be totally honest, isn't exactly my cup of tea, but I was going through what you might call a rough spot and was willing to read any-thing I could get my hands on.

In this mystery, the narrator herself ended up being the villain, but you didn't find that out until the very last chapter. I saw it coming a mile away, mind you, but I went online to look at what the reviewers were saying, and most of them had been duped right up until the end.

I'm harder to surprise. Probably because I know just about every trick there is, every manipulative tactic, every method that exists for twisting the truth ever so subtly until reality itself bends to your command.

I didn't murder my husband.

I want you to know that from the very beginning.

But I thank God every day that he's dead.

TWO

Justine held her son's hand as they stood in line.

"How much longer?" West whined.

Justine tried hard not to snap. She'd made herself a promise to hold it together for her son. For West.

"This part can take a while," she reminded him, "but after we get through the line and go through the big machines, we'll find a spot by the window to look at the planes taking off."

As a toddler, West would have lit up at the idea of watching giant planes taxiing outside Logan airport. Now he was four and already jaded.

He shifted his weight from one foot to the other, yanking down on her arm.

Justine freed her hand and pulled out her cell, not because she had anything important to look at on her screen but because she needed to rest her nerves. It had been years since she'd flown anywhere. That was before she'd become a mother, and even those few short experiences hadn't been all that friendly to her anxiety. Now she had West to worry about, not only for his safety but also for her sanity and that of all the other passengers on their flight.

West was what his daycare teacher called "energetic," and Justine wasn't exactly looking forward to trying to keep her son entertained and quiet for the next five hours, especially not when she herself was so nervous about traveling.

West had been looking forward to this trip for months. During his four years on the earth, he'd never ventured beyond about a fifty-mile radius from their New England home. She wondered what he'd think about Detroit.

She wondered if he would hate it just as much as she once had.

It wasn't exactly Justine's idea to head

back to Michigan. When she moved away, she'd made herself a promise never to return, and up until now she'd remained true to her word.

Her husband and her therapist thought the trip was a good idea. A chance to get some kind of closure, maybe.

Or maybe the chance to tell her mother how much she hated her once and for all.

THREE

I'M NOT sorry that he's gone. I think it's important to get that out of the way. If I were to tell you all that he put me through … oh, well. The jury didn't want to hear the details, and I assume you don't, either.

That's fine with me.

But I don't want you to think I'm heartless. You can think of these pages as my confessions of sorts. I don't know. Maybe you'll burn them after you read them. That's fine with me.

As long as you read them first.

That's all I ask.

The jury didn't get to hear the entire story. I realize nothing I'll say here can change what already happened, but it's important for me to tell you that I'm sorry.

I'm not sorry he's dead, mind you, but that certainly doesn't prove that I'm the one who killed him. Did I think about it? Yes. Fantasize about it? Sure, but that's not breaking any law. You can't prosecute a woman for murderous thoughts. It's just not how things work in a free society. And yet here I am.

Here I am.

I didn't murder him.

I don't know if you're going to believe me or not. I don't blame you for hating me, for believing everything those newspapers wrote about me.

But I didn't murder him.

I loved him, in a sick and twisted way. I was lost without him. Entirely and utterly lost.

And I'm sorry for your sake that he's gone.

I didn't want to leave you so young. I didn't mean to abandon you like that.

But it wasn't my fault.

I've looked up details about the family that adopted you. Seem like nice folks. Salt of the earth kind of people. I hope they did right by you. I know it's too late now, but I would have liked the chance to thank them. For taking you in. For raising you right.

I wasn't ever planning on contacting you, but then I heard that your adoptive parents had passed. I was mighty sad to learn it, too. Here you are, barely in your thirties, and you've lost just about everyone.

I wish I could have changed things for you, but we've all got our own path to walk. Yours, I'm afraid, has been riddled with difficulties and pain, and for that I'm truly sorry.

You probably don't want to hear this from me, but I'm proud of you. Proud of the woman you've become, the mother I know you are. You love that boy. Trust me, I know it. And now that you're a mother yourself, I hope you can understand a little more fully why I did what I did.

How I ended up here.

That's why I'm writing you now. To tell you my side of the story. I know I might not be able to change your mind, but I want you to hear me out. Think about what I'm telling you. Then you can decide for yourself if that jury was right or wrong.

I want the chance to tell you my side of what happened. To assure you that I didn't murder your father. That's all I ask of you, Justine.

FOUR

"Come on, Mama," West prodded her leg as Justine fiddled with the strap on her boots. Why had she decided to wear her heels on a day like this? It wasn't as if she were trying to impress anybody back in Detroit.

Justine smiled apologetically at the man in a Seahawks hoodie waiting to go through security behind her. She and West were holding up the line.

"Come on, Mama," West repeated impatiently.

When Justine's husband booked tickets for their flight, she'd been adamant she wanted to travel during the day. No red-eyes for her, thank you very much. Now, she wondered if she'd made the wrong call. Maybe if West was dead tired, he wouldn't act up so much.

She squeezed her eyes shut as she finally managed to wedge her foot out of her tight shoe. Steve was supposed to be here with her. She needed his support. It wasn't her fault that the partners thrust this case on her husband at the very last minute.

"Good thing we paid for travel insurance," was all Steve said as he logged onto the website to cancel his ticket.

She couldn't believe he'd abandoned her like this. And why had she let him, anyway? She didn't owe her mom this visit. When Steve told her he couldn't make it to Detroit, she wondered if this was God's way of warning her to leave well enough alone.

She couldn't understand why she let Steve talk her into flying without him. Didn't he know how nervous she got on airplanes? No, she hadn't ever specifically told him she was scared of flying, but he must know by now. Wasn't that why he never suggested taking outlandish vacations in the Caribbean like so many of his colleagues at the firm?

She should have put her foot down. Told her husband that there was no way on God's green earth she was going to travel alone with their four-year-old son, especially not to Detroit. No way she was going to subject their child to the ravings of a madwoman. Not that West was going to come within a ten-mile radius of his grandmother, but still. Steve should have known how impossible it would be for Justine to make this trip without him. Not just emotionally but logistically as well. Did he have any idea how many daycare providers she had to screen in order to find someone to watch her son while Justine went out to talk to Alice? What if he hated it there? What if the daycare was dirty? What if there was lead in the water or something worse? The entire state of Michigan was falling apart. One of Steve's associates had even been called to Detroit as an expert witness to discuss that school where they built a playground on toxic soil. That kind of thing was happening all over the state. And Steve thought it was a good idea for her and her son to spend four days there without him?

He was as insane as Alice.

Justine set her boots on the conveyer belt and waited her turn to step through the full-body scanner. West was young enough they let him go through the gate after a cursory once-over with the wand. In ten or fifteen years, on account of his skin tone alone, he'd be stopped, questioned, harassed whenever he wanted to travel. It was part of life he'd have to get used to soon. Her son didn't realize how lucky he was to be so young.

For now, everything was new and exciting. He grinned widely at Justine as he waited for her on the other side of the full-sized scanner. She hated the machine, hated to think about whatever radiation might be coming out of it. She held her breath, reminded herself that there was nothing to fear, and stepped through security.

"Wasn't that cool?" West jumped enthusiastically as Justine tried to put her tight boots back on without losing her balance.

"Yeah," she mumbled. "Real cool."

"Will we get to do it again before we get on the plane?"

She shook her head and answered mindlessly, "Not this time."

Justine glanced back at the TSA line, which had only grown longer in the half hour they'd been waiting. First hurdle past. A hundred more to endure before this ordeal was finally behind her.

I DIDN'T WANT to disrupt your life. I can only imagine you meant it when you told me in no uncertain terms that you didn't want to have anything to do with me.

I'm sorry, Justine. I really am. I wanted to be a good mother to you. I wanted to give you the life that you deserved.

It sounds bad of me to say, unnatural somehow, but I think you were better off with those rich folks who took you in. I know it wasn't easy. I'm sure growing up in the suburbs had its share of hardships, but it was a better childhood than I could have offered you.

I don't regret what I did, Justine. I only

regret that it ruined any chance of having a relationship with you.

That's why I begged you to come and see me now. You probably don't know this. I made him promise not to tell you, but I've been writing to that husband of yours. The rich lawyer. He seems like a nice man, Justine. He really does. And I'm happy for you. For the life you've created and that little family of yours.

Your husband knows about my condition. That's the real reason I need to see you. Why it can't wait any longer.

I'm dying, Justine. Cervical cancer is no picnic even if you aren't serving a life sentence for murder.

I didn't want to tell you until I saw you face to face. But it can't wait. Doctors have given me a few more weeks, a month or two if I'm lucky. But given my track record, Justine, I don't put much stock into things like luck.

I told your husband. I didn't tell you. I was worried you'd think I was being manipulative. Conniving. But it's the naked truth. By this time next year, you'll be a complete orphan.

I'm sorry, Justine.

I would have liked to meet you again under more positive circumstances.

There's a journalist I've been talking to, nice young man from back East. We've been working together for the past year, putting together my story. I'm not allowed to profit from the sales, you know. That was part of the court order.

The journalist tells me that my book has bestseller potential. It's not even done yet, and he's already found some publishers who want me to sign on the dotted line. But I'm not going to do that until I get the chance to talk with you first.

You're the only surviving relative of your father's. That means anything I make from the sale of my story will go directly to you. I know you're not worried about finances. That husband of yours has you set for life, and I'm glad to hear it. I don't want to think of you and my little grandson suffering for lack of anything.

I'm not writing my book for the money. It's not for the infamy either. Trust me, I had my share of that during the trial itself. I'm sick of it all. But it's an important story to get out there. Might even help women in situations like mine.

I just want to clear my name.

I don't want you to live your life as the daughter of a murderess.

I want you to know what happened.

It's time for you to hear the truth.

SIX

WEST HAD EATEN every single French fry and licked each individual particle of salt from his McDonald's meal. With nothing but the discarded pickles from his burger left on his tray, he was already asking for dessert.

No surprises there.

If West stayed where he was on his growth chart, he'd be taller than his dad before he graduated high school. Steve had been a football star before a back injury kept him from playing college level. He was proud of the life he'd made as a Boston attorney, but Justine knew he still had hopes that West would follow in his athletic footsteps. Genes were on West's side, and if you could judge by their grocery bill, her son already had the appetite of a teenage athlete.

"Look, Mama." West pointed at a little bakery near their gate. "Donuts. Can we get some? I'm hungry."

Of course he was hungry.

Well, their flight wasn't scheduled to take off for another hour and a half. Dumping a ton of sugar into his system was probably easier now than trying to keep all his extra energy corralled until takeoff.

Justine picked up her purse, and West gave a preemptive squeal of excitement. "Think they've got sprinkles on them?" he asked while jumping from one foot to the other.

Justine was fumbling through her wallet, trying to decide if it would be easier to pay with cash or credit. West was so excited he started to dash out of the gate when he bumped into a white-haired woman wheeling her carry-on to a nearby seat.

"Be careful!" Justine snapped at her son. She reached out her arm reflexively to catch the old woman in case she stumbled.

"Oh dear," the stranger exclaimed. "I'm afraid I wasn't looking where I was going. That could have been trouble."

"No," Justine corrected and gave West an angry glare. "My son should have been more careful and should have remembered not to run when there are so many other people around."

West stared at his feet and mumbled a half-apology. Justine doubted the woman even heard.

"Are you all right?" she asked. The woman looked frail enough that a fall might have resulted in a broken wrist or worse.

"I'm fine, thank the dear Lord," she replied, dusting off her pants. "I'm just worried that I hurt your little guy there. Is he all right?"

"Yes." Justine was still upset with West and was debating whether or not she was going to keep him from getting any donuts after all. If he was still so hungry, he could eat a veggie tray or something that wouldn't send him into a sugar craze when he was already too energetic. When she'd convinced herself the stranger was fine and unharmed, she gave one last apology and prepared to leave, but the woman grabbed her by the hand.

"You have a lovely child," she said. Her

grip was twice as strong as Justine would have expected.

"Thank you," Justine answered, somewhat flustered.

"Children truly are a gift from the Lord, aren't they?"

Justine didn't know how to respond. It was a saying she'd heard before at church, but on days like this, she didn't exactly feel like West was as big a blessing as everyone else made him out to be.

The old woman smiled and let Justine go.

"I'll see you two soon," she said with an air of certainty.

Justine offered a noncommittal smile and took her son by the wrist.

"Ow," West complained, straining against her hold.

Justine made him apologize once more, and then she led him down the terminal in search of something to eat.

SEVEN

Dennis was a cruel man. A heartless man.

His lawyer did a good job keeping them out of the trial, but there were two exes willing to testify against him. To let the judge know how violent he was.

I was young, Justine. Barely eighteen when your father and I met. In his defense, I told him I was twenty-one. They used that at the trial, trying to prove I was dishonest. A pathological liar. The defense attorney grilled me for a full hour about the details of my age. Too bad he didn't spend a fraction of that time probing into Dennis's past abuses.

I don't mean to speak ill of your father. I've debated whether or not to tell you everything. I don't want you to worry that you've got a monster's DNA making up half of who you are. Because you're different, Justine. I know you are.

I'm not a well-off woman, not anymore, but I have my resources. I hired a female investigator to tell me what she could about you. To keep me posted. Once she even sent me pictures from my grandson's birthday when you took him to the swimming pool with all of his little friends.

I love that child, Justine. I'm sorry if you feel like I've been spying on you, and I hope you know I only did it because I love you so much. Your son is adorable. So sweet. So innocent.

So pure and happy.

I was like that once. At least I think I was. It's hard to remember now. But that's what I'm doing. Remembering so you can finally understand.

Dennis was eighteen years older than I was. My parents didn't like him, but I was raised to be an independent thinker. Strong and ambitious. In a way, I like to think that you inherited these same traits from me, just with a little bit of wisdom to temper that stubborn streak. A woman who's fiercely independent as well as sharp and intelligent, now that's a woman the world has to fear.

Sometimes I wonder who I might have become. What might have happened. I think some people could drive themselves crazy going down that rabbit trail for too long. But not me. I think about the what ifs, wonder how drastically different my life would have turned out, but you know what?

If I hadn't met Dennis, I would have never had you.

You're my gift to the world, Justine. You're my reason for living. You're the only hope I have that somehow, some way, God knew I needed my life to matter. Otherwise, I should have died the same night your father did.

EIGHT

Justine gave in and let West eat three donuts then bought him two puzzle books and a new headset at the outlandishly expensive airport electronics kiosk. She was probably spending extra money on him just to assuage her guilty conscience. While other happy families meandered by in the terminal to spend Christmas with relatives or embark on exciting vacations, she was traveling to Detroit with her son so she could dump him off at a daycare while she visited a woman she loathed.

Happy stinking holidays.

She didn't want to face Alice. Even now, she realized, she could take West's hand, walk down toward baggage claim, and leave the airport.

Steve might be a little upset, but he's not the one who lived his entire adult life knowing he was the offspring of a felon. Why in the world had Justine let him talk her into a trip like this?

Snow was falling outside. Part of Justine wished that they'd cancel her flight. If it got delayed due to weather, maybe she'd take that as a sign from God she shouldn't go to Detroit after all.

She wasn't a religious woman. Not as religious as her husband, at least. Steve had befriended one of his key witnesses last year, the leader of a big church in Cambridge who'd been shot by a home intruder. The pastor had invited Steve to Bible studies and Sunday sermons, and then all of a sudden Justine's husband was a walking, breathing Bible thumper.

It shouldn't bother Justine all that much. She believed in God, and she didn't argue when Steve wanted to take the family to church on Sundays. It was something she thought would be good for West anyway. But she couldn't help wondering if Steve's encouragement to visit her mom came as part of his newfound faith in this God of forgiveness, grace, and love.

Did her husband expect her to absolve a convicted murderer? There was a reason Justine's mom had spent nearly thirty years behind bars. Alice had deprived Justine of anything resembling a normal childhood. Alice had murdered Justine's father, robbing Justine of both her parents in one fateful blow.

In his spare time, which wasn't much to speak of, Steve had been going over details from Alice's case. In his mind, there was enough doubt regarding the circumstances that he thought Alice should have gotten herself a new trial. As far as Justine was concerned, there was nothing her mother deserved less.

Justine reached the gate over half an hour before her flight was scheduled to take off. There weren't any seats near the window, but West was far more concerned with his handheld game than he was at watching planes departing down the runway.

She found a seat next to two young women, one with her hair dyed a vibrant blue. It wasn't even noon yet, and Justine was exhausted from her day of travel.

You don't have to do this, she told herself once more. West might be disappointed not to go on an actual airplane, but she could always buy him a new game or toy as a concession.

She pulled out her phone, contemplating what might happen if she texted her husband right now. *Changed my mind. Staying home with West where we belong.*

The nice thing about Steve's newfound faith was that he yelled at her less than he had before he met that Cambridge pastor. He might be disappointed, might give her a disapproving sigh or two, but in the end he'd realize that the choice was Justine's to make and Justine's alone.

All she had to do was stand up, take West's hand, and explain to her son that their plans had changed. He'd be disappointed for a moment, but the promise of a trip to the water park or a gift of a new video game would melt away any permanent unhappiness.

She should leave.

And yet something in her heart was telling her to stay.

Was it possible she actually did want to return to Detroit? Was it possible there was anything Alice could say or do that would change what Justine thought about her mother?

Wishful thinking. That's all it was. The hope that once she saw her mother face to face, she'd realize that everything she'd read about the husband-killing monster was a lie. They'd hug. Embrace. Everything would be forgiven.

No, there was no possible outcome that involved the restoration of Alice and Justine's relationship. Nothing at all.

Justine took her son by the hand. "Come on, West."

He looked up at her. "Where are we going?"

She stood. "We're going back to see Daddy."

"What about the airplane?"

"Some other time," she answered half-heartedly. "Let's go."

NINE

You might be surprised to know that I'm a woman of faith now. I haven't made any big announcements to the press or anything. I told you before, I'm not in this for the publicity.

But my faith is real, and it's carried me through some of the most difficult times here during my sentence.

I hear your husband is also a Christian. I'm glad about that. God knows this life is hard enough even with his Word to cling to in times of trouble.

I don't want to preach at you, Justine. I really don't. But maybe one day you'll read these words and know in your own soul that they're true. I hope so. I pray so.

I don't have anything else in this life to cling to, which is probably why I've accepted my imminent death.

You don't want to have a relationship with me. I get that. I understand. I really do. But maybe once you've heard my side of the story you'll feel a little differently.

Dennis was abusive. I'm sure you're familiar enough with the court case to know that much at least. But it wasn't the physical blows, Justine. That's not what did us in.

I still have nightmares about it. Did you know that? One of the guards here makes fun of me. Tells me if I'm so filled with remorse that I wake up screaming I shouldn't have murdered my husband in the first place.

I tell her I'll pray for her. I think that really gets under her skin.

The screams and the nightmares aren't about your father's death. Not at all.

The nightmares are about being trapped. Do you know what it's like to be trapped, Justine? Stuck? I can't move. It's like trying to walk through cement that's dried up all around you. You thrash and scream and try to get someone to help you out, but the only one who hears your cries is the man who poured the cement on you in the first place.

And he laughs.

Just throws his head back and laughs in your face, his breath hot, his palpable evil unbearable.

Laughing in your face.

People thought we had a perfect marriage. That's what's so distressing about the entire thing. If he hadn't been a TV personality, if there hadn't been a two-million-dollar life policy in place, if we'd been ugly or poor or from the wrong side of town, nobody would have cared when he got himself killed.

But that wasn't the kind of couple we were.

I knew when I married a newscaster as popular as Dennis that I was subjecting myself to the public eye. I thought I knew what that meant. Thought I was ready. I was expecting some rude remarks, some comments about our differences in age or race.

I was even prepared for words like gold-digger and trophy bride getting thrown around. That's just what happens when a young, attractive woman marries a millionaire who's twice her age, right?

Well, Justine, I have news for you. There's a reason a man like Dennis went through three other exes before settling on me. And there's a reason his first wife attempted suicide (on more than one occasion) and why his second underwent a very public mental-health breakdown.

I should have seen the warning signs, but I was mesmerized. When we met, I was nothing but the intern, the minimum-wage employee whose job was to dress smartly and show up with Dennis's coffee just the way he liked it. You probably don't have to use your imagination all that much to picture what it was like when he lavished me with so much attention. Smothered me with gifts. Paid down my credit cards and set me up in one of the nicest apartment complexes in Detroit.

I was young and stupid, but that's no excuse. I should have known better. I did know better. Right before we got engaged, I even tried to call things off. He tapped my home line. Can you believe it? He'd got it into his head that I was flirting with the weatherman, and he actually paid to get my phone tapped in order to try to prove I was cheating.

I told him we were done, and that's when he showed me his true self. He reminded me about how much debt of mine he'd paid off. He knew lawyers, plenty of lawyers. It was either stay with him or get myself sued.

I should have let him bankrupt my savings account. Instead, I let him destroy my very soul.

Tapping my phone, it turns out, was only the beginning of Dennis's madness. Once we were married, it only got worse. Following me to the store. Hiring his employees to track my whereabouts. He made up stories about crazy stalkers who were sending threatening letters to the news station and told me I couldn't go anywhere without protection.

It wasn't a bodyguard he hired for me. It was a prison guard.

A year into our marriage, I couldn't leave the house. He told all our friends I'd had a nervous breakdown. Told my parents I'd been diagnosed as agorophobic. Eventually convinced a doctor to prescribe drugs that kept me foggy, placid. Just the way he liked me.

You were the best thing that ever happened to me, Justine. When I found out I was pregnant, I felt for the first time in years like I had something to live for. A reason to exist. A reason to survive.

Dennis didn't want children. I know it's terrible to tell you this, but you have to know the truth. Dennis had no desire to become a father. I had to hide the pregnancy from him. Starved myself in hopes I wouldn't show. I couldn't tell the doctor I was expecting, but I was terrified the pills would hurt you, so I'd take them while Dennis watched then force myself to throw them up.

You deserved so much better. You have no idea how terrible I feel when I read scientific studies that talk about prenatal health. I did what I could to take care of you. God knows I tried, but all I could do was keep your existence hidden from your father for as long as I could.

But Dennis found out anyway.

Of course he did.

And that's when everything went from bad to horrible.

TEN

"Why are we going back home?" West
protested.

Justine had to practically drag her son as
they made their way toward the airport esca-
lators. "You don't need to worry about that,"
she answered. "All you need to know is we
changed our plans. Sometimes that happens." She was trying to decide whether to
offer him more junk food or a trip to the
video game store as a concession. Either one
should be enough to settle him down and
prevent a tantrum here in the airport.

At least she hoped so.

"I thought we were going to visit Grandma." West pulled against her grip with all his
strength.

"Alice is not your grandma," Justine snapped. She pulled West toward her and whispered in his ear, "Listen, I'll explain more in the car, okay? But right now, I need you to be a big boy and do what I tell you."

West didn't budge. "I want to go see Grandma!" he screeched.

"Hello there, young man. Did you lose somebody?"

Justine blinked at the old woman, trying to remember why her face looked familiar.

The white-haired passenger smiled at Justine. Great. The same little old lady her son had nearly plowed over in the terminal.

"Is everything all right?" she asked.

Justine let out her breath. No, everything was not all right, but that didn't make it this stranger's business.

Justine was about to pick up her son and carry him out of the airport kicking and screaming if necessary, but the old woman was rummaging through her oversized purse.

"Does your son have any allergies?" she asked Justine. "I have some farm-fresh goat-milk chocolate here and would be happy to share if that's all right with you."

West's eyes had already widened at the

promise of candy. There was no way Justine could deny him now. "That'd be fine," she replied with a resigned sigh.

She hoped the woman would catch from the tone of her voice that she didn't feel like a long, drawn-out conversation.

"My name is Lucy Jean, but I insist on being called Grandma Lucy." The woman shook West's hand then extended hers to Justine.

"Nice to meet you." Justine made a show of glancing at the clock above them. "West, say thank you for the candy, and then we've got to go."

"Where are you flying to?" Grandma Lucy asked.

West stuck out his lower lip, and Justine knew he was preparing to give this stranger his best impression of a sob story. "We were gonna see my grandma," he began, his voice trembling slightly, "but now my mama says we can't."

Grandma Lucy frowned. "How disappointing." She turned to Justine. "Was your flight cancelled? That snow's really coming down, isn't it?"

So far, Justine hadn't been able to give West a compelling reason why they were leaving the airport, but she figured the weather was a as good an excuse as any. "Yeah," she responded quickly. "It's really too bad."

"Where does your grandma live?" the old woman asked, bending down to address West as if Justine weren't even there.

"In Detroit," he answered, and Grandma Lucy's face lit up.

"Really? Well, that's where I'm headed too. In fact, they've been calling standbys at the gate." Grandma Lucy pulled out a ticket, and Justine realized she and the old woman were booked on the same flight. Grandma Lucy smiled warmly. "I bet we can get you on board if you really wanted to."

West's face brightened, and Justine was convinced he would have taken Grandma Lucy's hand right there and gotten onto the plane whether his mother followed them or not. She really had to have more in-depth discussions with him on stranger danger.

"Come on, Mama." He grabbed Justine's sleeve. "Let's go on the plane."

Justine didn't move. She didn't want to give in to her son, didn't want to reward him for throwing a tantrum. She thought about how disappointed her husband would be if she took West home right now, then she looked at Grandma Lucy. There was something calming about her presence. The woman's confidence and familiarity unnerved her, annoyed her to no end, and yet Justine felt somehow drawn toward her.

"Come on, Mama." West wrapped his arms around Justine's waist. "Let's go to our airplane. Please?"

Justine let out her breath. There was something inexplicable about this stranger's presence that felt both inviting and unwelcome. As her eyes moved from Grandma Lucy to West, Justine knew as certainly as she knew that it was snowing outside or that she loved her son more than anything else in this world that she was meant to get on that airplane. Call it destiny, call it whatever you want, but Justine knew in that instant as this little white-haired lady smiled at her warmly that she and West were supposed to fly to Detroit, and no amount of nerves or fear or protests could get her to change her mind.

ELEVEN

AFTER KEEPING my secret for nearly the entire pregnancy, Dennis had finally figured it out. You have no idea how hard your father's lawyers had to fight to keep the jury from hearing this part of the story.

I'll spare you the details. Suffice it to say, your father reacted as deplorably as I thought he would, and about an hour later, I was in the ER getting ready for surgery. I was hemorrhaging. They weren't just worried about your health. You and I both nearly died that night.

You were delivered by emergency C-section. Your father couldn't come in the room, and the OB who delivered you begged me to call the police.

"You don't have to pretend that you fell down the stairs," he told me. "I know what happened. I've seen this kind of thing before."

He was giving me a way out. Telling me he'd call the police for me if I was too scared to do it myself. Promising me they'd help me find a safer life, a better life for me and my daughter.

He didn't know who I was. Didn't know who I was married to. Didn't realize that no matter where on God's green earth I took you, your father would hunt us both down. Dennis didn't want a child, but now that you were here, he wasn't about to let you go. Not without the fight of our lives.

And so I told that nice doctor I really had fallen down the steps. Thanked him for saving your life. Told him there was nothing at all he had to worry about.

He was older, probably in his sixties when he delivered you. Most likely, he's dead by now. I think about him, wonder what might have happened if I'd listened to him. Allowed myself to believe he could help the two of us, desperate as we were.

You were in the hospital for several weeks. You had to put on weight and learn how to nurse before we could bring you home. Overnight, Dennis turned into the father of the year. He even got permission to bring in a camera crew to the hospital and introduce you on TV to the greater Detroit area.

"My little miracle baby," he called you. And it was true. Back then, they didn't have as fancy care for babies born that premature. The doctors told us you had a fifty-fifty chance to survive.

And survive you did.

Your father was a monster, but nobody knew it. People sent in gifts from all over the state. That's how much they loved your father. The newspaper wrote you up as the most famous baby in all of Michigan.

Nobody knew your father was the reason you were premature.

Nobody knew it was your father's fault you and I both nearly died the day you were born.

Nobody knew it was going to get even worse before I could find a way to deliver you permanently to safety.

TWELVE

"How old are you, young man?" Grandma Lucy asked West. The old woman hadn't left their side since Justine headed to the gate with her son.

"I'm four," he answered, beaming proudly.

"Four? Wow. You're awful big for your age."

West grinned at the apparent compliment. Justine wondered how it was that adults could make comments like that about children's body size and shape without it coming across as aggressive or rude. She also didn't appreciate how Grandma Lucy was addressing West and not herself, but to be fair, Justine hadn't done much more than an-swer the old woman's questions with mono-syllables.

"And are you a Christian, West?" Grandma Lucy asked, leaning in toward him. "Do you know Jesus as your personal Lord and Savior?"

Good grief. Was this eccentric stranger really about to start preaching to a preschooler?

"We go to church," Justine inserted sharply. She adjusted the strap of her purse, trying to decide if there was time to get West one more snack from McDonald's before they had to board.

"Not every week," West started to protest, but Grandma Lucy didn't seem to hear him. She was addressing Justine directly.

"Oh, there's so much more to having a personal relationship with Christ than just showing up to church on Sundays."

Justine was finished. It was bad enough Steve had changed so much over the past year, droning on and on about Jesus this and God that. Last summer, his pastor's wife had given Steve a kids' Bible to read with West at bedtime. Justine was certain her husband would let the habit die after the first few nights, but here they were, months later, and he was still going at it strong.

Justine didn't mind that West was learning Bible stories and going to church. And she couldn't deny that her husband was infinitely easier to live with now that he had "come to God." But even though he never stepped right up and said so, Justine got the feeling she was a constant disappointment to her husband, that he'd be more in love with her, happier with her if she got into this whole Jesus thing as much as he did.

Maybe he'd prayed this annoying old woman into their lives. Maybe Steve asked God to send them someone persistent who'd pester Justine until she finally got as serious about her faith as Steve wanted her to be.

Justine was spared the need to end the awkward conversation when the flight attendant invited passengers traveling with small children to board. West wasn't a toddler anymore. Justine didn't have a stroller or booster seat or any clunky baggage to take on the plane with them, but she wasn't going to sit here and listen to some stranger proselytize, either.

"Come on, West." She took her son's hand and let out her breath. "It's time to get on the plane."

THIRTEEN

You were a beautiful child. I don't know what happened to them, but I had boxes and boxes of pictures of you when you were a baby. You weren't even six pounds by the time we brought you home, but you were strong. You were a fighter.

I was so proud of you.

You gave me a reason to live, Justine. If it weren't for you, I ... well, you don't need to hear that side of it.

For the first little bit after you came home from the hospital, your father and I got along. He seemed to have changed his mind about not wanting to be a dad. I think part of him just liked the attention he got because of you. But there was a part of him, however small, that loved you in his own way.

Your father had demons, Justine. I'm not sure I mean that in the literal sense of the word, but he didn't necessarily want to be a monster. I don't know what went wrong with him, and it's too late now to try to figure out anyway.

You had just started crawling when the beatings started again. Dennis was taking me to different doctors, telling them that I was unstable. Post-partum psychosis, they called it. I'm sure you've heard of it.

I wasn't depressed. I wasn't crazy.

I was a prisoner.

Dennis found a doctor who prescribed me something horrible, something meant for people with severe mental illnesses. It knocked me out. Made me gain fifteen pounds the first two months, and that's on top of all the weight I gained during the pregnancy. I couldn't nurse you anymore. Could hardly function.

He took me to more doctors. Complained about my behavior. Hinted I might not be safe around our child. Hired a cute, perky au pair to move in with us and "help out with the baby," as he put it. Really, he just wanted someone to take to bed since I was so drugged up and overweight by then he'd lost his interest in me.

I'm ashamed to admit it, but I was relieved when he found another focal point for his attentions.

The drugs kept coming. You kept growing. Dennis told the au pair all kinds of terrible things about me, made it sound like I couldn't be trusted alone with my own child. She took you out and about every day, leaving me alone. Nothing to do but cry and beg God to end my life.

I could have done it, but I held onto the hope that if I managed to get myself healthy, Dennis would let me be your mother again. I did everything he told me to do. Ate nothing but cabbage soup for weeks on end because Dennis told me I was fat. Took my meds, not having a clue that my problem wasn't a mental illness but that my husband was drugging me to keep me compliant.

I don't know what happened to the au pair, but she disappeared. Dennis told me her mom was sick and she flew back home, but she'd told me she was an orphan. Truth be told, I bet he killed her. They'd gotten into a terrible fight the night before. I heard him yelling at her.

The next day she was gone.

Of course, I can't prove anything. When I mentioned it at the trial, the judge told me to shut up. Said it had nothing to do with the case. I think it had everything to do with the case. I was scared for my life. If Dennis could make an au pair simply disappear, a woman nobody came looking for, a woman with no connections or legal representation, what could he do to me? He'd already gotten multiple doctors in his pocket, men who testified that I was unstable, unfit to be a mother.

Dennis controlled every single aspect of my life. And the nightmare was far from over.

FOURTEEN

Justine and West were seated in the same row as a sharply dressed businesswoman. The passenger introduced herself as Meredith then went back to the journal she was writing in. Justine watched Grandma Lucy board and felt relief when the old woman headed toward the back of the plane. Something about Grandma Lucy's pointed questions and intense gaze left Justine feeling terribly uncomfortable.

Well, here they were. On their way to Detroit. The more she thought about it, the more Justine couldn't shake the feeling she was meant to be here. Did that mean she was meant to visit Alice as well?

Justine might not be as into church as

her husband was, and she certainly wasn't the type of person to go evangelizing in an airport like Grandma Lucy, but she believed in God and wondered if it was his voice telling her to go to Detroit after all. But why? Did she need some kind of closure with her bio mom? What had the woman done for Justine other than give her birth? It was because of Alice's murderous rage that Justine had spent years in the foster system before getting adopted. It was because of Alice's notorious mental illness that Justine had spent years in therapy, paralyzed with fear that the monster that had taken over her biological mother might be lying dormant in her as well.

Why did her husband, God, and the entire universe seem to be conspiring to get Justine to visit this woman?

Alice was unhealthy. Steve had let it slip. Justine had no idea her husband was in communication with that felon. Why in the world hadn't he told her sooner? But Alice was sick. Maybe even dying. She wanted to see Justine.

The trip had made sense when Steve first arranged it. A family trip to Detroit. See some of the area Justine remembered before her adoptive family moved to the East coast. Take West to the Children's Museum and the zoo.

But now with Steve working, there was nothing about this trip that felt like a vacation.

And yet here she was.

You chose this, Justine reminded herself. She and West could have walked out of the airport. They'd been close to doing so when Grandma Lucy grabbed a hold of them. Justine wasn't some prisoner being held hostage on a flight she hadn't agreed to take. She was here because at some point, she and Steve decided it would be a good idea, and at some point in the past hour, a fluke encounter with a stranger in the airport made Justine change her mind about going back home with West.

She was meant to be on this flight. She knew it.

But that didn't mean she wasn't worried. What would Alice say to her? What if Justine met her mother, saw her infamous insanity up close, and that woke up the dormant demons she'd inherited from that monster?

She wouldn't let West come anywhere

near his grandmother, but what if this trip had some kind of negative impact on him anyway? Alice's negative energy seeping into her son.

She was overthinking things. She had to stop. The flight attendant began her safety speech about seat backs and tray tables. Justine checked West's seatbelt to make sure it was buckled snugly, then she shut her eyes, let out a deep breath, and tried to force her anxious body to relax.

He died on a Tuesday.

I remember it was Tuesday because that was the only morning he went into work a little later, not hours before the sun rose.

He couldn't find the cufflinks he wanted. Thought I'd left home and sold them. Accused me of pilfering money away so I could leave him. Even suggested I'd given them as a present to a secret lover.

He was raving around the house, shouting like a lunatic, throwing drawers open, telling me he'd find my stash of cash and kill me.

You were asleep in your room. You poor, sweet angel, you'd learned to sleep through anything.

As hard as life was for us, you were a happy little girl. You were chubby once you started growing as a baby, but as soon as you learned to walk your muscles turned lean. I think you spent one day toddling and after that you took off running. Running through the house, laughing, yelling, giggling.

You had no idea your father was a monster.

You had no idea your mother was insane.

You were blissfully unaware of the danger we were in.

But I wasn't.

The truth was I hadn't sold your father's cufflinks, but I had been making plans. You'd gotten an ear infection right after your second birthday. I took you to the doctor. Your father came too. Didn't trust me out of the house with you. He was afraid I'd run off.

But he couldn't follow me into the bathroom at the children's clinic. That's where I saw the poster. A toll-free number women could call if they were in an abusive relationship.

I didn't have a pen or paper. Your father didn't let me travel with those. He was too scared I'd write someone a note begging for help, and then the picture-perfect prison he'd created for me and you would collapse and crumble around his feet.

I didn't have a pen, but I had my mind. And I stared at that poster, burned the numbers into my head.

I couldn't use the home phone to call for help, but I knew if I kept that number memorized, I'd make sure that once I got the chance I'd use a pay phone. One day, I was certain, your father would slip up. He'd stop for gas when I was in the car, and I could jump out and race to a pay phone. Or he'd forget to lock us in the house like he always did when he left for work, and I'd walk nonchalantly over to the neighbor's and ask to make a call.

I knew my fantasies were stupid. Knew your father would never be so careless. But memorizing the number made me feel strong. Made me feel brave.

At night, I'd lie awake holding imaginary phone conversations in my head. Telling the compassionate woman who answered the toll-free number that my husband kept my daughter and me locked in our house. That a year ago he'd killed our au pair and had managed to do so without raising a shred of suspicion. That he kept me placid and compliant by threatening to kill our daughter, this perfect little angel who was the only reason I had to live.

I'd tell her about the drugs. "He says I'm crazy," I whispered in my mind, "but I never had any problems like this before we got together."

And she'd explain to me what deep in my soul I already knew. I wasn't insane. I wasn't psychotic. The drugs were part of my prison. With them, Dennis knew I couldn't think clearly. Couldn't fight back.

"You should stop taking those pills," the imaginary woman would tell me.

And so I did.

Dennis didn't find my stash of cash that morning. He didn't find any love letters linking me to this imaginary lover. He didn't find the cufflinks he was sure I'd stolen.

What he found was much, much worse.

SIXTEEN

Justine was thankful that West was on good behavior. He ate a few snacks then settled down to watch an in-flight movie. The relative calm gave Justine the chance to try her hardest to relax.

Unfortunately, it also gave her the chance to be alone with her thoughts.

As each minute brought their plane closer and closer to Detroit, Justine felt the stone in the base of her gut churning, growing sour. She had to consciously focus on her breaths to keep from hyperventilating.

"Just because you share her genes doesn't mean you're going to become anything like her," Steve had told her years ago. Justine was pregnant, terrified that she would turn into the same kind of villain as her mother.

And thankfully, for then at least, Steve had been right. Justine's transition into motherhood was one of the most blissful, delightful surprises that had ever happened to her, as natural and as powerful as falling in love.

As it turned out, she wasn't defined by her genes.

When West was an infant, she held her breath, wondering if her descent into insanity would take her by storm the second her son started crawling or walking or speaking.

And then West turned one and next two. Still no depression, no hint of psychosis. The anxiety was always there, but not to the point where Justine couldn't control it.

By West's third birthday, Justine felt like she could finally let out her breath. She'd made it. Hadn't attacked her child or her husband. Hadn't slipped into a murderous, psychotic rage and tried to destroy the ones she loved most. At that point, she gave herself permission to stop worrying so much. Permission to forget about the woman who brought her into the world.

And then a few months ago, Steve told her Alice had contacted him.

"She's changed," he said, his eyes and tone begging her to believe him. She couldn't understand. Why in the world did he want her to give this woman any chance to get close to her or her family? Even the fact that Alice had contacted Steve should show she was just as manipulative and conniving as she'd always been. Why hadn't she contacted Justine directly if she really wanted to talk?

In the end, Justine attributed her husband's actions to his newfound faith. Didn't Christians believe in grace and forgiveness at all costs?

It wasn't until she'd had that dream that she even considered making the trip to Detroit.

It was just before Halloween. Justine had volunteered all day for the costume party at West's daycare. She was tired. A little grumpy. The next day was Sunday, and she knew her husband would try to wake them up early to go to church. Couldn't she sleep in just one day of the week?

That night, she dreamed that she saw Alice trapped in some kind of haunted carnival ride. Her mother was screaming for help, begging Justine to find her. To save her.

Inside the mansion was nothing but mirrors. Each time Justine thought she saw Alice's face, it was her own image staring back at her.

Until she got to the far wall. She saw the door, knew she had to open it, knew she was going to open it, knew that once she did open it, her life would be ruined.

Even as Justine sat next to her son on the flight to Detroit, she could remember staring at her own hand as it reached out for the doorknob. Slowly turned and pushed it open.

Alice was inside, her clothes covered in blood, her face distorted by both insanity and rage.

The knife in her hand was dripping. Disgusting.

The body at her feet wasn't Justine's father.

It was West.

She'd woken up screaming for her son. Even when Steve tried to calm her down, she couldn't stop hyperventilating until she brought her son into bed with them, held him in her arms. Even once she'd managed to convince her logical brain that West was safe, she still couldn't control her breathing, couldn't stop her arms from trembling, her mind from replaying the sense of foreboding she felt as she pushed open that door.

"I think you need to see her," Steve told her the next morning. She thought he was the crazy one until her therapist repeated the exact same sentiment the following day.

Justine still wasn't convinced. It wasn't until a few weeks later when she had another dream, the one that finally changed her mind.

It was the same haunted castle. The same freaky mirrors.

But there was no door this time, no bloody knife, no stabbed son.

Instead, it was Alice, lying on a bed, holding a little doll and crying. "Where'd she go?" she wailed over and over. She reached out her arms, and for a split second, Justine wanted nothing more than to bury her head against this frightened woman's chest and tell her everything was okay.

"Where'd she go?" Alice repeated, her voice so pitiable Justine woke up with tears on her cheeks.

"I think you need to see her," Steve repeated the following day.

And Justine knew he was right.

Now, she wasn't so sure.

In her early twenties, Justine had poured over every single newspaper article she could find dating back to her father's murder. He'd been a beloved TV reporter, which meant the trial made national news. The story had every ingredient of a good scandal for the time. Her father was white, handsome, somewhat famous, and several decades older than Alice. Alice was black, young, and beautiful, with well-documented mental instabilities and quite a few motives to kill her aging husband. Before their wedding, Alice had fallen into a heap of financial troubles, financial troubles that all went away the moment she signed her marriage license. As far as the public was concerned, Alice had every reason to be profusely grateful to her husband, who gave her all the material possessions she could desire as well as the best medical care for her mental illness that money and fame could buy.

But she wanted more.

A jury member said that he probably would have acquitted her if it hadn't been for the fact that Alice had taken out three separate life policies on both her husband and their daughter just a week before the killing. That and the fact that the detectives found letters from a secret lover, a lover urging Justine to end her marriage and live with him forever.

Justine read the reports and realized her mother wasn't just greedy and insane.

She was also stupid.

Fringe groups still believed Alice when she upheld her innocence, in spite of all the evidence against her — her well-documented mental disorder, her secret lover, the multiple life insurance policies. Alice's supporters argued that the all-white jury and the racial tensions of the time would have made it nearly impossible for her to get a fair trial. And yet her sentence was upheld after multiple appeals, her requests for parole were repeatedly denied, and Alice was doomed to spend the rest of her life behind bars.

Justine didn't want to admit it to herself, didn't want to sound like an ignorant child unable to look at reason. The facts of the trial could hardly be any clearer. Alice had killed her husband. She had even attacked

Justine. The scar on Justine's thigh where the knife blade went into her leg was a daily reminder of her mother's criminal insanity.

And yet Justine had to wonder. It was a question she'd never dared to mention to Steve, to her therapist, even to herself except for when she was at her most open, her most honest, her most raw.

Part of Justine wanted to visit Alice. Part of Justine wanted to hear her mother's side of the story.

Part of Justine was dying to believe her mom was as innocent as she claimed.

SEVENTEEN

I'D HIDDEN the pills in a sewn-in pocket of a purse I never used.

Dennis found them anyway.

I'd been off them for nearly a month. I was finally starting to feel like myself again.

A week or two earlier, and he would have killed me for sure. But not that Tuesday morning. I was thinking more clearly than I had in years. I felt like me, not some zombie toy of his.

And I knew I had to save you.

Save my little girl at all costs.

Your father had never hurt you before, Justine. I want you to know that. In spite of how wicked and evil he was, he never caused you any type of physical injury. Even when he threatened to, it was only to keep me in line.

Dennis shoved me against the wall. He threatened to force-feed me all the pills at once, spelled out how long and painful my death would be if he did. He tried to shove them down my throat, so I bit his hand.

I knew it was dangerous, Justine. I really did, but he'd never hurt you before. I thought he was bluffing when he pulled out that knife.

He wanted me to overdose. He'd already called two of my doctors and told them I'd threatened self-harm. A week earlier, he dictated a suicide letter and made me transcribe it. That wasn't the first time. And still, I wasn't nearly as scared as I should have been.

Then he began to tell me all the other steps he'd taken to make sure my death looked deliberate. The phone calls he made from our home line to the suicide prevention number. The type-written diary pages he'd forged to make it look as though I'd been planning my death for months.

There was a time when I would have welcomed death. But then on that fateful Tuesday morning, you woke up and came plodding down the stairs. You were wearing blue fuzzy pajamas, the kind that cover your feet and zip up the front.

You were so beautiful, Justine, and I knew that I had to live. What kind of life would you have if I let your father kill me? How long would it take before his lust to inflict pain destroyed you as well?

I couldn't let him do that.

He had the knife in his hand. Said he'd kill you if I didn't take the pills. Told me that he'd filled out paperwork in my name, taken out life insurance on our little baby.

"Take those pills, Alice," he said to me, "or I'll kill our little girl and tell the police it was you."

I knew he had the resources to make that happen. I hadn't heard about the life insurance policies until then, but I remember him forcing me to sign some papers a few weeks earlier, when I was still detoxing from the drugs and couldn't think straight.

He had the knife up to your neck. You looked at him and smiled. You thought he was trying to tickle you.

He underestimated how much stronger I was now that the drugs were out of my system. Now that not only my own life but my daughter's was in danger.

You should never underestimate a mother's fury. Her innate instinct to protect.

I did what I thought I had to do, Justine. I'm so sorry you got hurt in the process.

Your father is dead. I killed him that morning. I'm not sorry I did it.

It was the only way to keep us safe.

It was the only way to keep you alive.

EIGHTEEN

THE INCIDENT HAPPENED SO QUICKLY, it was over before Justine realized it had started.

Before she realized how much danger she was in.

"He's got a gun!" a passenger shrieked.

A scuffle. Someone got knocked out. And then a man stood up, waving a gun in the air.

Justine wasn't even sure if she had blinked. What was going on? She was supposed to feel scared. Logic told her it was the opportune time to panic, but she was too stunned to react at all.

"The people of Detroit have failed our kids," the man began. For a second, Justine thought this was some kind of drill. A false alarm. Something staged.

Then the palpable fear that enveloped the entire cabin told her the danger was terribly real.

"What's going on?" she whispered to the woman beside her.

"I think that's the air marshal." Meredith gestured toward the man who had been knocked out in the preceding scuffle.

Justine clutched her son, hoping to somehow shield him with her body from the terror in the cabin.

"I think it's a hijacking," Meredith whispered.

"But why?" Justine had the feeling her brain should be keeping up, but it simply couldn't. "Who is he? Why is he doing this?"

"He calls himself General," Meredith answered. "Says he's doing this for the kids of Detroit. I really don't understand it either."

West was clinging to Justine's side. She kept his body pressed against hers, hoping she wasn't suffocating him in her attempts to shield him from the danger surrounding them.

Justine didn't react when Meredith took

her by the hand. Somehow it felt calming to have another woman by her side. The physical touch was comforting.

"I'm going to help you protect your little boy," Meredith whispered, and Justine felt tears of terror stinging her eyes. Protect her little boy? Did that mean this man might possibly try to hurt her son?

The gun was probably a prop. That was the easiest thing for Justine to believe. A prop so he could get what he wanted, gain some notoriety, and then the air marshals or traffic control or whoever took over in cases like this would find a way to get all the passengers safely on land.

But how? The air marshal was knocked out. Maybe even dead. Who was going to protect them? Who was going to keep any of them safe?

"Mama," West whined, and Justine tried to shush him.

"Not now, buddy. Just be quiet and still." The last thing she wanted was for West to make noise, to alert General to his presence. As long as General was focused on his tirade, as long as he kept talking into the cell phone cameras the passengers were pointing at him, he would ignore her son. She was thankful West was in the window seat, hoping that her body was large enough to keep him hidden from sight.

"He's only four." Justine's eyes filled with tears. Did God hear her? Did he see? Her little boy was only four. This wasn't something a child his age should ever have to endure.

Meredith squeezed her hand once more. "It's going to be all right," she whispered, but Justine couldn't bring herself to believe it could possibly be true.

NINETEEN

THE KNIFE WAS in my hand. The life was draining out of Dennis's eyes.

"You know you'll pay for this," he hissed. Even as death stood by waiting to escort him to judgment, your father tried to terrorize me. "Those insurance policies weren't just for the girl. You know how bad this will look."

I didn't know how bad it would look. How could I? How could I have guessed that just like he made preparations so that my death would look like a suicide, he also made contingencies so that I'd be the primary suspect if he was killed?

Which is exactly what happened.

It wasn't just the new insurance policies,

although those certainly didn't help my case.

There were the forged love letters from some anonymous boyfriend. The police found them stashed away behind the liquor cabinet. They immediately suspected I was having an affair, even though they never found out who the mysterious man was.

Because there was no other man, Justine.

No other man at all.

Then there was Dennis's journal, which he only kept at work. He'd written in it for over a year, notes about how worried he was about my health, how he kept trying to protect me but was afraid I might one day hurt our daughter. He made up imaginary scenarios about coming home and finding you with bruises on your body, bruises I couldn't adequately explain. The au pair wasn't mentioned at all. I imagine if the police ever found his journal, Dennis didn't want them trying to find her for questioning or digging too deep into her disappearance.

Of course, Dennis had been carrying on with multiple affairs. I wasn't surprised, but his journal spelled out how I'd discovered love notes from his girlfriend two nights before he died. How mad I'd gotten. How I'd threatened to kill him and our daughter both because I was so angry.

The doctors who testified at trial didn't help my case, either. It didn't matter that for every single office visit, Dennis had gone in with me, planted firmly by my side like an all-loving husband. Had told me what kind of symptoms to claim I had. Often, he injected me with something before I met with the physicians. I still don't know what it was, but there were times I couldn't even remember the appointments after I got home.

In the end, the prosecutors didn't need anything else. I was a woman, a minority, a gold-digging trophy bride with a boyfriend on the side, a history of insanity, and a well-documented diagnosis of post-partum psychosis which made me dangerous to my daughter.

I knew I didn't stand a chance at the trial.

I was right.

They even tried to blame me for the cut you got on your leg while your father and I were struggling with the knife. It didn't help that I couldn't tell them how you got hurt, if the knife was in my hand or your father's at the time. You know how it ended. First-degree assault and child abuse for your injury. First-degree murder for your father's death.

Two consecutive life sentences.

I imagine that when you read the news articles about everything that happened, you think I'm a monster for what I did. I don't know what I have to say to get you to believe me, Justine, but there's something else I need to tell you.

I'm dying. The doctors doubt I'll see much past New Year's. I've made my peace with my sentence. I've made my peace with God.

The only hope I have left in this world is that you can hear my story, look me in the eye, and tell me you believe me. That's all I ask before the good Lord takes me home.

TWENTY

"THE PEOPLE of Detroit have failed our kids."

General's loud voice carried throughout the entire cabin, over the hum of the engine, over the pounding of Justine's pulse raging in her ears.

"They've sold our children's souls to the devil, building their school on toxic land."

That's what this was about? The elementary school with lead in the soil? Justine remembered her husband mentioning the case, but surely it wasn't reason to murder.

Was it?

"Five minutes," General was saying. "The governor has five minutes to call me on my personal cell phone before I'm forced to do something desperate." His gaze swept up and down the cabin. Justine's stomach flopped like a fish out of water when his eyes locked onto hers. It only lasted for a fraction of a second, but it was long enough to freeze the blood in her veins. Her entire body went cold and numb.

"Five minutes," General repeated. "Five minutes before a hostage dies."

Justine held West close. Now instead of using her body as a shield so the shooter couldn't see him, she covered West's face with her hands so he wouldn't try to turn and witness the violence erupting all around them.

Justine couldn't believe it. Surely the God her husband spoke about so lovingly, so reverently wouldn't allow something like this to happen. Not to her. Not to her little boy.

Justine's heart pounded in her ears. For a minute, she was afraid she was going to be sick.

Seconds passed. The wait was an eternity. Was this the definition of purgatory?

The air felt thinner. Had the captain done something to the pressure system?

Were they going to suffocate before General could kill them all off one by one?

General continued to pace the aisle until a single beep sounded from his phone.

"Time's up."

He walked up to a flight attendant. The woman was visibly shaking. Justine couldn't pull her eyes away. She kept her son shielded as best as she could as General pointed his gun at the flight attendant's head.

They were too far away for Justine to hear what he was saying. In her state of paralyzed shock, Justine convinced herself the entire scene was a giant bluff.

When the reverberating sound of gunfire deafened her ears, she realized how wrong she was.

The flight attendant dropped lifeless to the ground, her body heavy, the sound of its thud sickeningly solid. Final.

West dug his fingers into the flesh of Justine's belly and started to cry. Justine pleaded with God to keep him safe. It didn't matter what happened to her. It didn't matter what happened to anyone else on this doomed flight. Just as long as God protected her son.

"She's dead," a woman screamed, her announcement to the cabin entirely unnecessary. There was no way anybody could have survived a shot to the head at such a close range.

"Five minutes," General repeated. "Five minutes before another hostage dies."

TWENTY-ONE

You learn a lot serving out a life sentence. Did you know that?

Like not all criminals are evil. Sometimes desperate people do desperate things.

I was safer in prison than I ever had been under Dennis's roof. If not for the stress of the trial itself and the knowledge that if the jury found me guilty I'd never see you again, I could have felt perfectly at peace.

I gave my life to Christ right before my sentencing. There was a Bible study for the women prisoners. I started going, desperate to give hope or meaning to the terror I'd lived through.

It was in prison that I learned how to pray. Of course, anybody can pray when their husband's beating them up, but my new kind of prayers were different.

I prayed for all the other people Dennis had hurt. Asked God to heal their wounds and show them grace.

I prayed for the jury that found me guilty, the prosecutors who spread vicious lies about me, the public that devoured the scandal like vultures descending on roadkill.

But mostly, Justine, I prayed for you. I prayed that God would place you in a good home, that he would help you to feel loved and cherished and safe. When I heard that one of your foster families wanted to adopt you, I was thrilled. I'd already been sentenced by then, and even though I was looking into appeals, I was starting to realize there was no way I'd ever leave my cell. Your father was just too smart. The life insurance policies, the journal he kept at work. He knew that one of us was going to die, and he made provisions to make me out to be guilty no matter which of us it was.

I'm glad you inherited that money. I prayed that your new family would use it well. By all accounts, it sounds like you've done well for yourself. I'm really glad about that. And I know it's a lot to ask, Justine, probably too much, but I would certainly love to meet my grandson before the Lord calls me home.

TWENTY-TWO

Justine hadn't realized she was still clutching Meredith's hand beside her until the muscles in her fingers started to cramp. General's timer beeped again.

Five more minutes had passed.

"What's he doing?" West asked. Justine didn't have any answer for her son.

General was still in the back of the plane. It should have been good news. It meant that he was farther away from West. But Justine couldn't keep herself from staring as he waved his gun at another young woman and told her to stand up.

"What's your name?" he demanded.

"Willow," she answered. Her hair was blue. Beautiful in various shades, all the way from teal to azure. She looked a little familiar. Where had Justine seen her before?

"Are you following what's going on at the schools in Detroit, Willow?" General's voice was low. Menacing. Like a snarling dog warning another animal to keep its distance.

"A bit," the young woman answered.

"They're building playgrounds on toxic land." His volume increased, and his voice became more animated as he spoke.

Maybe, Justine thought, just maybe if he kept rambling, it would give the other passengers the chance to figure out some plan of attack. Maybe …

"They're poisoning our children, and they don't care."

The young woman's lip trembled. Even in her seat so many rows away, Justine was convinced she could hear the girl's throat working to swallow.

"I'm sorry that I have to do this." General raised his gun and took aim.

Justine willed her eyes to squeeze shut.

"Let her go." The strong voice echoed throughout the entire cabin. It sounded as if the engines themselves had all shut off to help Grandma Lucy's words carry throughout the airplane.

She was so short, she didn't even come up to General's shoulder, and yet the little old lady stood glaring at him until it felt as if General's body shrunk a full foot and a half.

"What do you want?" he asked, but there was confusion in his voice. Weakness.

"I told you to let that young woman go." Grandma Lucy took a step forward. West finally managed to squirm free and turn around in his seat, but Justine was too engrossed in what was happening in back of the plane to tell him to stay down.

"Why would I do that?" General snarled.

"Because she's young, and you don't want to take another innocent life."

There was a filling, soaring sensation in Justine's chest. Had she been holding her breath this whole time? Now that Grandma Lucy stood to confront the hijacker, Justine could finally remember how to breathe.

"This is the only way to get anyone to listen to what I have to say." General sounded desperate. Scared. Like he was about to lose control any minute.

If the passengers could just find a way to communicate with each other, all it would take was a few strong bodies to bring him down.

Please, God.

Prayers rushed through Justine's soul in the same hurried, unexpected way her breath had returned to her lungs at the sight of Grandma Lucy's boldness. Her body felt warm. Ready for action. Ready for something to happen.

But what?

Grandma Lucy stepped in front of General's gun. "If you need a victim that badly," she proclaimed, so loudly that her words seemed to echo and reverberate off the walls of the cabin, "you can take me. I'm more than willing to meet my Maker."

General stared at her as if considering, placed his hand on the trigger of his gun, and shrugged. "Fine." The menacing growl was back in his voice, and his stature had regained its former confidence. He took a step forward until his gun was just an inch from Grandma Lucy's forehead. "Have it your way, old hag."

TWENTY-THREE

They say that confession is good for the soul. I'm afraid if I tried to list out every single sin I've ever committed, I'd never finish this letter to you. Early on after my sentencing, I visited with the chaplain quite a bit. He kept asking me if I regretted killing my husband.

I'm sorry, Justine, but that's the one thing I can't apologize for.

I've forgiven Dennis. That much I can say.

But I'm not sorry I killed him. If I hadn't, he would have destroyed me and you as well. I've searched my Bible, and I've begged God to change my mind if I'm wrong, but I can't regret the fact that he's dead.

The chaplain said that's a sign of unforgiveness. I told him he's never had to kill anyone to save his little girl.

I don't mean to tell you I've lived a perfect life. I struggle every day with anger at the men on that jury who put me here. But I can't change what's past. I can only try to make amends for the future.

I've already told you I'm dying. I don't know how much longer I have, but sometimes as I'm drifting off to sleep at night, I can hear the heavenly music that soon is going to call me home.

I know you might read my words and decide I'm making it all up. You've read about your father's journal, how manipulative he said I was. I imagine that there's part of you that wants to believe I'm innocent and another part of you that might always harbor doubts.

I can't prove to you that anything I've said here is true. I can't make you believe that killing your father was the only way to save our lives. You've read about me online, I'm sure, and have probably already come to your conclusions about who I am and what my motivations were and how reliable of a witness I am.

Just remember, Justine, that looks can be deceptive. Your father had everyone fooled — the doctors, his coworkers, his friends. The jury. Except I have no proof to offer you. Nothing conclusive to guarantee my innocence. God alone knows what really happened. He is my witness as well as my judge. I'll admit there are times when I wake up from terrifying nightmares. I've just died, and God tells me I can't come into heaven because there's blood on my hands. And I pray and I plead and I ask him to show me grace. I wake up crying.

I believe God will judge me justly when my time finally comes, and I rely on his grace to cover all my mistakes. I know you aren't all-knowing like the Lord, but I couldn't die peacefully thinking that you believe a lie about me, about who I was, about why I did what I had to do.

My conscience, my soul, my eternal destiny are in God's hands now. All I can ask is that before I go home you hear my story.

Then I can die and finally be at peace.

TWENTY-FOUR

General stared at Grandma Lucy, aimed his gun at her head, and pulled the trigger.

Click.

Nothing happened.

General's eyes widened.

"His gun doesn't work!" The shout from the back of the plane was followed by confusion. Chaos.

"Get him."

"Grab him."

"Careful."

A skirmish. Loud grunting. Someone punched General in the face.

He fell.

Several more shouts, and then it was over.

"We got him!" someone yelled.

And that was it. General was bound, his gun now pointed at his own chest. Passengers let out a collective sigh of relief. In the seat beside her, Justine heard Meredith offering a short prayer of thanks. The captain made an announcement that they'd be landing in Detroit soon.

"You think you've won?" General shouted with a guffaw. "You're all going to die."

Justine chose to disregard the ominous threat. It was the ravings of a madman. Nothing more.

"Mama?" West asked.

Justine wrapped her arms around her son, ashamed that in her fear and then relief she'd momentarily forgotten how scared he must be.

"It's okay," she whispered, tears streaking down her cheeks. "It's over. They caught the bad guy, and we're okay."

General's laugh still echoed throughout the cabin. "You're all gonna die."

Justine ignored his words, hugged her son close, and thanked God for keeping them alive.

TWENTY-FIVE

"I'm gonna kill you both." That's what Denis told me. That's what I believed.

I've talked with the chaplain about it quite a bit since I've been here. Told him that the only thing I feel guilty about is that I don't feel guilty.

Am I a sociopath? Am I the monster the media made me out to be? The monster I'm sure you believe that I am?

He would have killed you, Justine. As sure as I know you're my daughter, sure as I believe God will usher my soul into heaven to stand in his presence any day now, I knew your father meant to kill us both.

I couldn't let that happen.

If you had never been born, I wouldn't

have cared. I would have given up years earlier. But you were so little, so beautiful, so perfect. You loved me. Trusted me.

And you loved him too. Your innocence was completely unaware of the pure evil that lived inside that man.

I took the knife. How could I watch while he slit open your throat? How could I sit by and do nothing?

I took the knife, and in that moment, I knew.

Either I would survive, or Dennis would.

There was no way he and I were both going to come out of this alive.

And since my brain was working for the first time since your father put me on those drugs, since I had the adrenaline surge that comes when a mother watches her child in danger, I did what I had to do.

Your father's attorney and the judge were right. I shouldn't have run away after that. Shouldn't have taken you in the car with me and tried to skip town. I didn't even realize you were bleeding until we were halfway to Toronto. We had to stop, had to get you medical attention.

If it hadn't been for that, I like to think we might have made it across the border.

I used to spend a lot of time thinking about that scenario. An alternate reality created entirely in my mind while I sit here, cold behind these metal bars.

We make our way to Canada. I smile and tell the border agent we're going to do some shopping. Smile at him nicely, make small talk about exchange rates.

I don't know a single person in Toronto, but it's a big enough city that we manage to get by. I go to one of those women's shelters, take you there with me, explain that we're in danger. I left my ID, everything I had at home.

Eventually, we learn to start over. I get a job working as a nanny for a rich family. They have a little girl exactly your age, and the two of you become best friends. We go to church. I teach you about the Lord. We pray before meals and sing songs in the car.

Life is beautiful, Justine.

And we never, ever talk about your father again.

TWENTY-SIX

Justine couldn't believe it was finally over.

The captain announced they were just minutes away from Detroit. The first thing Justine did when they landed would be to cancel her return flight and rent a car to drive back home.

There were a dozen emotions she should be experiencing. Relief that the danger was past. Fear for what her son witnessed. Guilt that they had survived.

Curiosity and confusion. Why hadn't the gun gone off? Was it the old lady's prayers? Steve would tell her it was some sort of miracle. That God had saved her and West both. As glad as she was to be alive, if it really had been God's hand saving them, why hadn't he protected the other passengers just the same?

Justine's body was trembling, but she wasn't cold. It wasn't until West reached up to touch her face that she realized she'd been clenching her jaw.

"Mommy?" he asked.

Justine's heart nearly broke in two at the sound of her son's sweet and innocent voice.

"Yeah, baby?"

West started to turn around in his seat. Justine held him so he couldn't look behind and see the signs of violence in the aisle.

"Mommy?" he repeated, squirming in her grip.

Justine didn't let go. "What is it?"

"What's that smell?" West asked.

This time Justine did turn and saw a billow of smoke filling the back of the cabin. An alarm started to blare, deafening her ears.

Please, God, no, Justine begged as the passenger behind her shouted in a shrill panic, "Fire!"

TWENTY-SEVEN

Your leg was cut. To this day, I don't know how it happened. I'm so sorry about that, Justine.

We had to go to the hospital. I tried to come up with a story. You were standing on a chair. You wanted to chop veggies like you'd seen Mommy doing. You tripped. You fell.

The doctors didn't believe me.

I started shaking uncontrollably when they brought the policeman in. At first, he thought he was questioning me in a case of suspected child abuse. He had no idea I'd just ended your father's life.

But the truth came out.

I suppose it always will. At least, that's what the Bible says. Still, I like to indulge myself in daydreams from time to time, think about that nice lady in Toronto who might have hired me as a nanny, think about her imaginary little girl who would have become your best friend. It's not what actually happened, but I've dreamed out the details so vividly I can tell you the scent of the family's laundry detergent, feel the matted hair of their beloved little puppy, a mutt who's just as endearing as ugly.

I'm sorry that's not the life I could have given you.

I'm sorry I couldn't tell you my story sooner.

I'm just glad that soon you'll be here, that I'll be able to explain to you what really happened, apologize to you for all the mistakes I made.

I can't believe I'm about to look at you face to face. I just pray God gives me a few more days, that my body holds out a little bit longer.

I need you, Justine. I need to tell you the truth. That I never would have deliberately lifted a hand against you if my life depended on it.

That I loved you so much I would have done anything — yes, even kill — to keep you safe.

TWENTY-EIGHT

SHE HAD to get her son away from the smoke. But where could they go?

The Detroit skyline was in view, but all Justine could see was a jumble of chaos as men and women scrambled out of their seats in an attempt to get toward the front of the cabin.

The screams of the passengers melted together with the shrill screech of the siren. Justine held her son close. "Don't leave me," she shouted into West's ear, but even then she wasn't sure he heard her.

They were so close. How could so many things go wrong on a single flight? It didn't make sense. General's last words reverberated in her mind, as well as his horrid laugh. "You're all gonna die," he said. Was he the one who planned this? But how could he have set the entire plane on fire when he was tied up in the back of the cabin?

The question of how the fire started didn't matter. The only thing that mattered was whether or not Justine could save her child. How much longer until the plane landed? And would Justine survive that long to keep West safe?

Terror and chaos swarmed around the cabin as passengers shoved one another their scramble to get out of their seats. Justine gripped her son's arm even more tightly. She was about to lift him up in her arms when she remembered that you were supposed to get low when there was smoke. But how could they get low without being trampled to their deaths?

"West, be careful," Justine shouted as someone plowed into her from behind. She lost her balance. Tripped. Her breath was stolen away as someone stepped on her back. She couldn't breathe.

Where was her son?

"West!" She reached out her arms, flinging wildly. Someone lifted her up to her feet. The smoke was so thick she couldn't even see the face of her savior.

She lurched forward, blinded by the smoke, terrorized by the fear. She couldn't even see which way was the front of the cabin anymore. She could only assume that if she followed the swarm of panicked bodies she'd be heading away from the worst of the smoke. Not that she had any choice. Everybody pressed up against her. Even now that she was on her feet, the density of the crowds stole her breath away. Or maybe that was all the smoke.

But where was her son?

"West?" Justine tried to yell, but a coughing fit wracked her entire body. What if he'd fallen? What if he'd gotten himself trampled in the swarm of bodies?

"West!"

Somebody grabbed her arm. Justine couldn't see a thing, but the person was leading her away from the throng, toward the thickest of the smoke. Justine tried to fight them off. She needed to find her son, but she was so weak.

"West?"

She heard a faint cry and dropped to her knees. Tiny arms reached for her and flung around her neck. He was on the floor, crouching beneath a set of seats. Good boy. She felt his body, trying to assure herself he was safe, and in that moment she understood.

In the fire, in the chaos, in the terror she'd experienced on this flight, Justine had only one concern. To protect her son. To make sure that no matter what happened to her, West landed in Detroit alive.

She would have done anything. If General had come at them with the gun, she would have plucked his eyes out with her bare hands if it meant saving her child.

She wrapped her arms around her little boy, her lungs filled with too much smoke to form the sobs that promised sweet release.

"We're going to be okay," she told him, begging heaven to hear her prayers. "We're going to be okay."

TWENTY-NINE

CARRIE STEPPED into her patient's room. "Did you press your call light, Alice?" she asked, making her way toward the woman's bedside.

Alice's oxygen canula was a little crooked, and Carrie reached out to straighten it up. As she did, Alice reached up and took Carrie's hand, pointing at the TV screen in the room.

"What's going on?" the old woman asked in a rattly voice.

Carrie frowned. She and her colleagues had been watching the news at the nurse's station as it unfolded. "A plane hijacking," she answered, reaching for the remote. Her patient didn't have much time left. From what Carrie suspected, Alice's body should have given up days earlier. The only thing keeping her alive was the hope of seeing her daughter.

It was a tragic story, one the nurses all felt keenly. Alice had been incarcerated for the past thirty years, serving a life sentence for murdering her husband. Carrie had gone online to look up the details of the case. Apparently, the murder had been one of Detroit's greatest scandals of its day, and with good reason. Alice had taken out multiple life policies on her husband, then killed him before trying to flee the country with their little girl. Alice was a murderer, a felon, and a child kidnapper, and now she was trying to reconnect with the daughter she'd injured in her husband's fatal attack.

"Justine's coming from Boston to visit me," Alice announced each and every time Carrie came into the room. Carrie just hoped that her daughter knew what she was getting into. It was common knowledge on the hospital floor that Alice would say anything to get people to give her what she wanted.

Alice continued to stare at the screen even after Carrie had turned off the news.

At least one hostage had been killed, maybe more. It wasn't the kind of story an old woman on palliative care should worry about.

"Was that the flight from Boston?" Alice asked, her voice weak.

Carrie's stomach dropped toward the floor. Boston? It couldn't be the same flight Alice's daughter was on, could it?

"I don't think so," Carrie replied, but her uncertainty must have been obvious.

"Turn it back on," her patient demanded. "I need to see this."

"Alice," Carrie began, her voice softening, "I'm not sure it's such a good idea to …"

"Turn it on," Alice snapped.

Carrie obeyed. In spite of her patient's weakness, she thought she detected a hint of the same rage that so long ago had led the woman to cold-blooded murder.

Now, the news was even worse. A fire on the plane. The video footage panned over a tarmac studded with ambulances and fire trucks.

"See there," Alice announced, pointing at the screen. "Flight 219. From Boston. That's the plane my daughter's on."

Carrie patted the old woman's shoulder. There was no way that Alice could be certain of the exact flight number, could she?

"I'm sure it's something else," Carrie began, then let her voice trail off. The plane was about to land. Fire and smoke billowed from its back half. Carrie wasn't even sure how many passengers the medical crews on standby would find alive once it touched down.

"I don't think we should watch this anymore," she said, her voice low.

Alice didn't respond.

THIRTY

Justine's body had remained strong and vigilant. She knew that if they survived their landing, the passengers would be in even more of a frenzy to get off the plane. She vowed to shield West with her body even if the crowds ended up trampling her to death.

Anything to save her son.

The landing was awful. At one point, the plane tilted and threw Justine's head against the chair in front of her. Still, she held as steady as she could, promising herself and her son and God that she would protect West to her dying breath.

And then they were on the ground. EMTs and emergency personnel flocked in. "Take my son," Justine shouted at the first worker she saw. For the first time since the terror began, she allowed herself to willingly be separated from West. Her lungs were stained with smoke. She couldn't move a single muscle. The only thing that mattered was West's safety.

Eventually, someone else came and escorted her off the plane. She was so weak she almost had to be carried, and her legs gave out the moment they reached the steady asphalt. Justine scoured the crowds for her little boy. She saw him stretched on a gurney being attended to by two paramedics. One of them leaned over and laughed at something West said. Justine let out her choppy breath.

She had done it.

She had saved her son. God had protected them both.

Everything was going to be all right.

THIRTY-ONE

JUSTINE HELD her husband's hand. Ever since Steve landed in Detroit just a couple hours after she did, he hadn't left her or West's side. Even when the federal agents wanted to question her about the events that took place during the skyjacking, Steve refused to separate from her for even a few minutes.

She was thankful he was here. Glad for his support. Now, two days had passed since she landed in Detroit, but her lungs sometimes still stung from the smoke.

West was running up and down the hospital hallway. Justine had snapped at him once, but Steve reminded her that there were worse things her kid could be doing than expending a little extra energy.

Her husband gave her hand a squeeze. "You sure you're ready to do this?" he asked.

She nodded. Ready or not, this was why she had flown to Detroit in the first place. If she didn't carry through, her and West's traumatic experience would be for nothing at all.

"Do you want us to come with you?" Steve's voice was gentle. They'd had this same conversation multiple times before, and each time Justine's answer was the same.

"This is something I need to do on my own."

Steve gave her hand one last squeeze. "All right. I love you."

"I know." She smiled at him. She and Steve had gone through a lot of changes recently. Some of them good, some of them terrifying. She didn't even want to think about what it would be like once they drove home and Justine had to settle back into life as normal. What's normal after witnessing your son nearly dying in a plane crash?

She was already replaying all the conversations she'd have with her therapist. She should probably find someone for West to talk to as well. There was no way that kind of fear could be healthy for someone so young to keep bottled up. It wasn't healthy for anyone, as a matter of fact, no matter what age they were. Justine couldn't sleep at night without waking up in cold sweats, her lungs stinging with smoke, her stomach dropping as the plane from her nightmare crashed to the ground.

Well, maybe there was reason for optimism. After all, she and her therapist had spent so much time this past year analyzing Justine's mother. Maybe it would be nice to have a change. That was one way to look at it, at least. The other way to look at it was Justine had endured more than any human being should ever have to endure. When would God look down and decide she'd had enough?

"I'm gonna take the kiddo to get donuts from the cafeteria." Steve spoke quietly, but not quietly enough.

"Donuts?" West did a complete about-face and sprinted back toward his parents. "Are we getting donuts, Dad?"

Steve smiled and tussled West's hair. Justine noticed he'd been touching his son a lot more than normal these past two days.

Her husband gave her one last kindly gaze. "You ready?" he asked.

Justine nodded. Ready or not, she was here. She was going to do this.

She reached her hand to knock gently on the door of her mother's hospital room, then quietly let herself in.

THIRTY-TWO

"So she's been asleep for how long?" Justine asked.

"Two days," the nurse answered. She had introduced herself as Carrie, had explained that she'd been Alice's primary nurse since she arrived here for hospice care.

"Is it a coma?" Justine stared at the woman on the hospital bed. She looked so frail and weak. There was nothing to indicate that this woman had once been young, beautiful, and murderous.

Nothing to indicate she'd spent almost the entirety of her adult life behind bars.

"Not a coma," Carrie replied. "But she's very, very tired."

"Is she in pain?" There was an inexplicable lump in Justine's throat, which she did her best to ignore.

"I don't think so. In fact, she was pretty restless yesterday, but today she seems so much more at peace."

As if on cue, Alice let out a faint sigh. Justine looked, trying to decide if that was a smile on her mother's face.

"I think she knows you're here."

Justine had no idea how Carrie could make a presumption like that, but she didn't want to waste time arguing. No matter how well this nurse claimed to know her mother, the stranger's presence felt intrusive.

"Have a seat," Carrie said, pulling a chair up to Alice's bedside. "You can talk to her. There's no reason to think she can't hear you. Just press that call button if you need anything."

Justine's legs trembled slightly as she lowered herself into the chair. She hated that she felt so nervous. It wasn't as if Alice was going to wake up from her near-coma and try to stab her in the thigh like she had when Justine was just a toddler.

"One more thing," Carrie said, reaching for a tattered notebook on Alice's bedside table.

She passed the book to Justine, who reached out for it tentatively.

"Your mother wanted me to give this to you when you got here."

"What is it?" Justine asked, uncertain if she wanted to open up the pages.

"I'm not sure," Carrie answered. "But it was very important to her that you got it."

The nurse left, and as soon as she was gone, Justine wished she'd come back. She had no idea what to do, what to say. Should she tell Alice she was here? Try to hold her mother's hand? What good would it do if Alice was already unconscious?

Two days ago, Justine had been terrified of dying and losing her child to terrorists. Now, she was afraid of a little old lady asleep in a hospital bed.

Justine let out her breath. Well, if she didn't know what to say, maybe she'd let her mother's words fill up the silence of her soul. She opened up the notebook, and her hands started to tremble as she read the first line.

I didn't murder my husband. It's important to explain that from the very beginning.

Justine flipped ahead, trying to guess just how many pages in this notebook Alice had filled. How long had she been working on it? And was any of it true?

I didn't murder my husband, Alice repeated on the second line.

Justine settled in her chair then checked the time. This might turn into a very long day.